JANUARY IS FOR JACKSON

MOUNTAIN MEN OF MUSTANG MOUNTAIN

DYLANN CRUSH

EVE LONDON

Stay Wild!
Eve London
x

XO,
Dylann Crush

To the Match of the Month Patrons, especially...

Jackie Ziegler

Thank you so much for your support. We couldn't do what we love without you!

Dear Reader,

Thanks for picking up a copy of January is for Jackson, the first book in the Mountain Men of Mustang Mountain series! We can't wait for you to meet Jackson and Emma. If you love their story and want to learn more about Mustang Mountain, sign up for our newsletter here: http://subscribepage.io/MatchOfTheMonth.

XOXO,
Dylann & Eve

January is for Jackson

Her mountain man hero must make an impossible choice.

Emma

I've always been spontaneous, but this time I might have gone too far. Showing up at my brother's remote cabin to surprise him for his birthday seemed like a good idea. But he's nowhere to be found, the cabin's locked up tight, and a snowstorm's on the way. When his closest neighbor stops by, the gorgeous grumpy mountain man insists on taking me home with him until the storm passes. He's burly and bossy, but I can tell there's a kind heart buried under the layers of flannel.

Jackson

The last thing I need is to be snowed in with my best friend's little sister. If anything happens between me and the beautiful curvy blonde, he won't just end our friendship, he might even end me. It doesn't matter that she's impossible to resist. The sooner I get her out of my cabin, the better off we'll both be. But how can I let her go when I know deep down she's meant to be mine?

Welcome to Mustang Mountain where love runs as wild as the free-spirited horses who roam the hillsides. Framed by rivers, lakes, and breathtaking mountains, it's also the place the Mountain Men of Mustang Mountain call home. They might be rugged and reclusive, but they'll risk their hearts for the curvy girls they love.

CHAPTER 1
JACKSON

IT WASN'T EVEN NOON YET, and I'd already had a hell of a day. As I peered at the Nelson's Mercantile sign through the dirty windshield of my half-ton pickup, I eased my grip on the steering wheel. Based on the dark gray clouds rolling in, Mustang Mountain was going to get another storm today. If I wanted to grab the rest of my supplies and get back up the mountain before the snow started falling, I needed to go inside and get this over with.

The bell over the door jangled as I entered the store. Ruby and Orville Nelson had been operating the Nelson Mercantile for decades. Their family history with the tiny Montana town went back almost as far as mine. That was about the only thing we had in common.

Ruby was hellbent on breathing new life into Mustang Mountain, while I was more than content with the slow pace and peaceful life. She thought if she could get some of the guys around here hitched, it would breathe new life into our struggling town. I hadn't stepped in when she hosted a women's weekend, and I looked the other way when she gave away free stays for girlfriend getaways at the two cabins she owned. This time, she'd taken it too far.

I held the postcard with my picture plastered across the front in my hand. She must have snapped it last month when I stopped by their place to chop some wood and make sure they had enough firewood for a while. Up here on the mountain we took care of each other, though that was about to change now that I'd seen how she repaid the favor.

"Good morning, Jackson." Ruby beamed at me from behind the counter. "Can I get you a cup of coffee?"

I stomped the snow off my boots and stalked toward her. "What the hell is this?"

She glanced down at the postcard. Her eyes widened a tiny bit, but she covered her surprise with another one of her bright smiles. "I suppose you were bound to see it sooner or later."

"Seeing as how you've got them plastered all over town, I suppose I was. What were you thinking?"

"I was thinking we need to bring some new families into town if we don't want to end up like Wolf Canyon." She set her hand on top of mine and her voice softened. "You, of all people, should know what kind of trouble we're in, Jackson."

Ruby might look like a kind-hearted grandma who

spent most of her time baking cookies and knitting Christmas stockings, but she had the mind of a shrewd CEO. Too bad my family hadn't hired her when business at the lumber mill we owned took a turn for the worse.

"And how is me appearing half naked on a calendar postcard going to bring families to Mustang Mountain?" I slid my hand out from under hers and crossed my arms over my chest.

"We need women." Ruby shrugged. "All you boys living up on the mountain by yourselves—"

"I told you to stop playing matchmaker. No good's going to come from that."

She tilted her head and studied me. "If you want this town to survive, we're going to need to bring in new residents. With the lumber mill closing, folks have been forced to move away to find work."

I clenched my jaw. No one felt worse about the lumber mill closing than me. "I did all I could."

"Of course you did, honey." She held my gaze for a beat, then turned and poured a cup of steaming coffee. "Coffee's on the house today."

"I want all of those postcards taken down by this afternoon." Even though her heart was in the right place, I wouldn't stand for having my picture plastered all over town. I hated being the center of attention. That's why I'd built a cabin halfway up the mountain where I could live in peace and quiet.

"It's too late." She peered up at me over the rim of her own coffee mug.

"What do you mean, it's too late?" My gut twisted and turned as I tried to imagine what she might have done.

"I can gather the ones we have left around town, but I already sent them out to everyone on the visitor bureau's list."

My hands clenched into fists. I'd never hurt a woman, but dammit, I wanted to hit something.

"You should feel flattered. I've already booked a few groups at the rental cabins. They can't wait to come to Mustang Mountain and see if they can meet their own mountain men."

"I'm not going to stand by and let you get away with this." I'd need to get the rest of the guys together. If she'd made me Mr. January, no telling who she planned to target next.

She cocked a hip and leaned against the counter. "I don't expect your gratitude now, though I bet you'll be thanking me when my direct mail campaign brings you the woman of your dreams."

"That's where you're wrong." I put my palms on the counter and leaned closer to her. "The woman of my dreams doesn't exist."

It about killed me to leave the mug sitting on the counter untouched, but she couldn't buy me off with a steaming cup of coffee. I didn't know what she had planned, but the guys and I would put a stop to it. Ruby Nelson might be a force to be reckoned with, but she was no match for a dozen of Mustang Mountain's toughest men. We liked our privacy, relished the remote lifestyle we led, and would do anything to keep it that way.

I sucked in a few breaths of clean, crisp air on my way back to my truck and pulled up our group text. Miles was ice fishing up at Lake Bliss, but hopefully, the rest of the guys would be able to get together.

> Me: Ruby's at it again. We need to get together soon. Who's in?

The message failed to send. Service must be out because of the storm. The sooner I got back up the mountain, the better off I'd be.

My truck slipped and slid on the snow-packed roads as I made my way away from town. There were only two cabins this far up the mountain: mine and the one belonging to my buddy Miles. Usually, one of us would get out and plow since the town didn't have the resources to maintain all the roads. With Miles out of town, that job fell to me, though I didn't plan on going anywhere for the next few days. He'd be out of town until next weekend, so there was no rush to get out and take care of the road. As long as I could get home, I'd leave it for later.

I paused as I passed the turnoff to his place. Fresh tire tracks in the snow meant he'd either come home early or someone was snooping around. We didn't get visitors, which meant the group who'd been on a breaking and entering spree might be targeting my best friend's cabin. I pulled into the drive to block them in, then grabbed my shotgun from the rack behind me.

His drive hadn't been plowed for a few days, so the snow reached halfway up my calves. I stuck to the tracks left by whatever vehicle had pulled in and crept toward the cabin. A big SUV sat halfway up the drive, wedged against a snowbank. One set of footsteps led toward the cabin. My grip on the gun eased. I could easily handle a single perpetrator.

As I turned the last bend and the house came into view, I squinted through the falling snow. A woman, no more than five feet tall, stood on the porch, her back pressed against the side of the cabin. I followed her line of sight across the clearing to where a huge gray wolf stepped out of the woods.

I WAS GOING TO DIE. All I'd wanted to do was surprise my older brother for his birthday, and now I was going to be eaten alive by a wolf. I should have known better than to visit northern Montana in January. Should have paid attention to the weather report playing on the radio, too. Then maybe I wouldn't have gotten the SUV I'd rented stuck in the snow. I should have done a lot of things, but it didn't matter now.

The wolf was huge, bigger than the ones I'd seen back home at the San Diego Zoo. Even from this distance, I could tell it had to be at least three feet tall at the shoulders. Knowing it would most likely be the last thing I'd ever see, I still couldn't help but marvel at its wild beauty.

It moved closer, one slow step at a time. If I'd stayed on the track team, maybe I'd have a chance at making a run for the truck. Who was I kidding? This short, curvy girl had no chance of winning against a tortoise, much less one of nature's most successful predators.

I pressed my back against the outer wall of my brother's cabin. When he didn't answer, I'd tried all the doors and windows. It was locked up tighter than Fort Knox, and knowing Miles, the windows were probably made of shatterproof glass. I seized the snow shovel by the door and prepared to fight for my life.

"He's not going to hurt you." A deep voice pulled my attention to the driveway, where a man made his way toward me through the deep snow. He had a shotgun hanging from his shoulder. Relief flooded through me. Maybe I wouldn't die today.

"You've got a gun. Shoot him!" My gaze shifted back to the wolf, who'd moved even closer. I could see the snow crusted on its muzzle.

The man laughed. "You want me to shoot a protected species?"

"I guess you'd rather have my death on your hands?" Unbelievable. I'd worried about my brother's decision to move to the middle of nowhere. If this was the kind of company he was keeping, I needed to convince him to come home.

"I told you, he's not going to hurt you."

"He's a wolf. I'm dinner. What part of that equation isn't making it through your thick skull?" My grip on the snow shovel tightened as the wolf moved even closer. He was only about a dozen feet away from the steps leading up to the porch. If he came any closer, I'd pee my pants.

"Hades, come here." The man held out his hand, and the wolf scampered toward him, gracefully leaping through the snow.

I let out the breath that had been lodged in my throat. "Don't tell me you have a pet wolf."

"No. Hades doesn't belong to anyone, but I took him in when he was just a pup. He's like a mascot for the town and was probably wondering why you're trying to break into my buddy's cabin."

With the threat of death by wolf mitigated, the reality of my situation took hold. "I came to wish my brother a happy birthday. Now that I'm here and he's clearly not, I realize how stupid that sounds. I tried to call, but couldn't reach him, so I figured I'd take my chances."

"Emma?"

"How do you know my name?" I squinted across the distance separating me from the giant mountain man.

"Hell, the last time I saw you, you were what, maybe seventeen?"

"Jackson?" There was no way the burly bearded man making his way toward me was my brother's best friend from college. Miles brought him home to Southern California for spring break during their sophomore year, and all my friends and I had drooled over him.

He climbed up onto the porch and swept me into a huge hug. "It's good to see you, Emma."

"It's good to see you, too." Too good. Though it couldn't be more than twenty degrees outside, my cheeks heated. I pulled back and took a good, long look at the face I always pictured as the hero of every romance novel I'd ever read.

He set me down but kept his hands on my waist. Even with his bulky winter gloves on, the pressure of his hands made my toes curl inside my thick, wool socks.

"What happened to you? You're all grown up." Dark brown eyes swept over my face.

My high-pitched giggle caught us both by surprise. I needed my nerves to settle. I also needed to get away from his embrace if I had any hope of pulling myself together. "Sorry, I guess I'm still a little nervous about having a full-grown wolf so close."

Jackson let his hands fall away and squatted down in front of the wolf. "Like I said, he won't hurt you. Hades, this is Emma. She's Miles's little sister, so be nice to her."

The wolf sniffed my gloves, then nudged his nose into my hip. I'd forgotten I'd shoved half a protein bar in my pocket earlier. "Can he have a protein bar?"

Jackson shrugged as he stood. "He'll let you know if he doesn't want it. He's a sucker for peanut butter."

"This one's peanut butter and banana." I pulled the half-eaten bar out of my pocket. The wolf sat down and waited. "Is he trained?"

"Not really, but he's always gentle when he takes food from someone. Just pull the wrapper off and put it in your palm."

I unwrapped the bar and held my palm out to the wolf. He looked up at me as he carefully took it from my hand and swallowed it down whole. "I can't believe I just hand-fed a wolf."

Hades rubbed against my hip, then took off toward the tree line.

"He knows a good thing when he sees it. What are you doing in Mustang Mountain?"

With the wolf gone, the rush of adrenaline started to fade. "I wanted to surprise Miles for his birthday. You don't happen to know where he is, do you?"

"Last I heard, he went ice fishing up at Lake Bliss. It's a half-day hike from here or about two hours on a snowmobile."

Dread swirled around in my belly. "He's fishing in this weather?"

"He caught a trophy lake trout last January. Now he can't stay away."

"Any idea when he might be back?"

Jackson bit down on his bottom lip. "I think he's planning on staying up there until next weekend."

The knowledge I'd made the trip from San Diego for nothing swept over me. "Great. I don't suppose you have a key to his cabin, do you?"

"Sorry."

I covered my face with my hands, determined not to break down in front of my brother's best friend.

"Hey." Jackson put a hand on my shoulder. "You okay?"

Why did I think it would be a good idea to come to Montana? If I wanted to get away, I should have booked a trip to a spa in Arizona or something instead of trekking all the way up here. If I had, maybe I'd be sweating in a dry sauna right now instead of freezing my ass off on the front porch of a remote mountain cabin. Not that I could afford a trip to a spa. I'd just about wiped out my savings by paying for a last-minute flight and renting the SUV.

Nodding, I swiped at my cheek and lowered my hands. "Yeah. I'm just sorry I missed him, is all."

"What are your plans?"

Good freaking question. My plan was to escape to my brother's cabin for a few days so I could figure out a plan. Getting laid off right after the holidays hit me hard. I hadn't had the guts to tell my parents yet. If I couldn't find a new job soon, I'd have to move back in with them... every twenty-five-year-old woman's dream.

"I guess I'll try to find somewhere to stay in town tonight. If you don't think he'll be back for a while, I'll head home tomorrow." My lower lip trembled, and I bit down hard to make it stop. I'd really wedged myself into a tight spot this time... and in front of Jackson, too. Not that he'd ever think of me as more than his best friend's little sister, but a stunt like this would guarantee it. It figured that my attempt at proving to myself

I could be competent and capable would turn out like this.

Jackson ran a hand over his beard. "You're not going to make it back down the mountain tonight."

The snow had started falling while we'd been talking. Giant flakes landed on his dark green hat. I couldn't feel my nose anymore. If I stayed out here a few more minutes, I'd probably end up with frostbite. The reality of my situation sank in.

"You'll have to come to my place." He didn't look too happy about it. His lips twisted into a scowl, and I could have sworn his jaw clenched under the thick layer of scruff on his chin.

I didn't want to put him out. Based on his sour expression, he looked like he'd rather stand out in the snow and freeze to death than take me home with him. The last thing I needed was to be forced to spend time where I wasn't wanted. I'd had enough of that at home.

"Don't you have a rope or something you can use to pull my truck out of the snow?" From what Miles had told me, Jackson had lived in Montana all his life. He had to be used to this kind of weather. It couldn't be the first time he'd come across someone stupid enough to get their car stuck in the snow.

"Yeah, but it won't do any good. I barely made it up the mountain myself. Until I get out and plow the road, there's no way you'll make it back down."

I tried to cross my arms over my chest, but the fluffy ski jacket I'd borrowed from a friend made it almost impossible. "When do you think you'll be able to plow?"

"Hopefully tomorrow. I'll try to get word to Miles too. He usually takes a satellite phone with him when he heads out alone."

Tomorrow. That meant I'd be spending the night with Jackson Hill. I got tongue tied even thinking about him. How would I be able to hold myself together overnight? My best chance of not making a bigger fool out of myself would be to limit our interaction as much as possible. I could say the trip drained me and head to bed super early. Or say I had a sore throat and couldn't talk so we wouldn't be forced to make conversation.

"I don't want to cause any trouble."

"No trouble at all. Besides, Miles would kick my ass if I let you stand out here and freeze to death." He held out a hand to help me down the steps of the porch. "Come on. We've still got a way to go up the mountain, and I'd like to make it before dark."

I grabbed hold of his hand and glove in glove, we walked down the steps toward an evening I'd dreamed about for years.

Too bad it wouldn't turn out like I'd always imagined. There was no way Jackson Hill would ever fall for a woman like me. Not when the idea of having to spend one night under the same roof made him look like he'd just swallowed a pitcher full of vinegar.

EMMA WAS quiet the rest of the way up the mountain. Thank fuck I'd arrived when I did. If something had happened to her... I didn't even want to think about it. I wasn't worried about Hades. He wouldn't have hurt her. But a million other things could have gone wrong. When I saw a woman standing on Miles's front porch, I thought it was the gal from Kalispell he'd dated for a little while. Hell, I wished it was. Then I wouldn't be on the way to my place with my best friend's little sister riding shotgun.

She was even prettier than I remembered. The last time I'd seen her had been at our college graduation. She must have been about seventeen with big blue eyes and the kind of curves that didn't belong on someone her age. The fluffy winter coat she had on now did a good job of hiding what was underneath, but I'd bet my favorite axe she'd only grown more beautiful over the years.

Thoughts like that would lead to no good. I flexed my fingers and adjusted my grip on the steering wheel. "Are you warm enough?"

"I'm fine, thanks."

There was only a foot of space between us, but it may as well have been an entire football field. Once we got in the truck, it seemed like she shut down. Probably the shock of being stranded on the side of a mountain in a winter storm. Though Miles had grown up in San Diego, he'd been living in Montana for the past eight years and was used to the elements. I didn't think Emma had ever lived anywhere but by the beach.

"I'll get the fire going as soon as we get to my place. That should warm you up." *My place...* I couldn't wrap my head around the fact that I'd be spending the night with Emma. Just the two of us. Alone.

Shit. I should have left the bed set up in the guest room, but my parents were the only ones who used it. When they both passed, I got rid of it so I could use the spare room as an office. I'd have to give her my room. Just thinking about her in my bed made my cock twitch.

"I'm fine, really." She stared out the window at the tall pines as we continued up the mountain. The minutes ticked by. I didn't know what to say or how to ease the tension that seemed to settle between us. Finally, we rounded the last bend, and I pulled into the long drive.

A huge snowdrift prevented me from pulling into the garage. The snow was falling faster than I expected. There was no way I'd get back out to plow tonight. Emma and I needed to be prepared to shelter in place for the next day or two. I'd been mentally preparing myself to spend one night together. How was I going to survive forty-eight hours with her in a one-bedroom cabin?

"Do you think Miles is okay?" She turned to me as I killed the engine. Her brows knit together and for a moment, all I could do was hope that someday someone would worry about me half as much as she was concerned about him.

"Yeah." I tried to offer a reassuring grin, but it had been so long since I smiled at anyone, it probably looked more like a grimace. "He knows his way around up there. I'm sure he's fine."

She nodded, and the crease between her brows disappeared. "Thanks."

"Ready to make a run for it?" I nudged my chin toward the front porch. "I need to come out and shovel before I can open the garage door. That means we need to go in the front."

"Do you need help bringing anything in?"

"I'll get my stuff. You just worry about getting inside and warming up. The door's unlocked, so head straight in."

She opened the door and slid out of the truck. I got out and walked around to the back to grab the couple of bags I'd picked up at Nelson's. I'd made it halfway to the front door when she screamed.

Dammit. I forgot to warn her about Moose. My

giant Rottweiler wouldn't hurt a fly, but she was a jumper. I dropped the bags in the snow and tried to get to Emma before the big dog knocked her over.

"Moose, no!"

Too late. Moose leapt up and Emma stumbled backward. She landed on her back and Moose took the opportunity to slather Emma's cheeks with her slobbery kisses.

"Get in the house." I shooed the dog away and grabbed Emma by the front of her coat. Hauling her to her feet, I checked for injuries. "Are you okay?"

"You could have warned me I'd be attacked when I opened your front door." Snow stuck to her long blonde hair. She wiped her cheeks with her gloves.

"We don't get a lot of visitors around here, so she doesn't know how to behave around strangers." I tried brushing the snow off Emma's back. Her jeans were going to be soaked through. "Once you get inside, you can change into..."

We both seemed to realize our mistake at the same time.

Emma's eyes rounded. "My suitcase."

Being around this woman was turning me into a complete idiot. My brain seemed to have lost its ability to function. "I didn't even think to grab it from the SUV."

"It's not your fault. I should have realized..." She closed her eyes like she needed a moment to compose herself. Then she took in a deep breath and opened them again. "It looks like I'm going to be completely at your mercy. Hopefully, you have a pair of old sweats or something you can loan me?"

Fate had a wicked sense of humor. Not only would Emma Bradshaw be sleeping in my bed, it seemed she'd be wearing my clothes while she did. "Of course."

Her lips spread into a hesitant smile. "Thanks, Jackson. I know this is a huge imposition, but I really appreciate you taking me in. I promise not to get in your way. I'll be so quiet, you won't even know I'm here."

The deep belly laugh worked its way up my throat, but I covered it with an awkward cough. Even if she didn't say a word to me for the next twenty-four hours, I'd still know she was nearby. Every nerve ending in my body had been on high alert since the moment I realized it was her standing on her brother's front porch.

I followed my footsteps back to where I'd dropped the grocery bags. It didn't matter how attracted I was to Emma. She was my best friend's little sister. He'd beat the shit out of me if he even suspected I was thinking about her.

And if he ever found out what those thoughts entailed... how I pictured cupping her cheeks between my hands and sucking her full bottom lip into my mouth... how I imagined running my hands over the curve of her naked ass... how I pretended her hands were sliding up and down my cock when I jerked off... I shivered.

He'd cut off my balls.

She was off limits. My head knew it. I just had to convince my dick.

I stomped my feet on the porch before stepping into the front room of the custom cabin I'd built with my own hands. It had been a long time since I'd had a visitor up here. Even then, I'd never had a woman in this space. I tried to see everything through Emma's eyes.

The first floor was an open concept, with a living room leading right into the kitchen and a small eating area that took advantage of the view. A floor-to-ceiling stone fireplace stretched to the vaulted ceiling and a set of wooden steps led to the second floor, where the primary bedroom and bathroom were. Though it lacked the sense of comfort and warmth my childhood home held, it was perfect for me.

"Let me get a fire going." I set the groceries down on the kitchen counter and pulled off my gloves and coat. "I'll take your coat."

Emma had shed her boots at the door and unzipped her coat to hand it to me. I reached for it, and our fingers brushed. A zap of awareness zipped up my arm at the contact, sending my heart into overdrive.

"Thank you." She didn't appear to be affected. If she'd felt the same shock, surely she would have shown some sign.

Whatever was going on between us was one-sided. I didn't know if that made me feel better or worse. "Make yourself at home."

"How long have you lived here?" She tilted her head back and gazed up at the vaulted beams.

"About six years. I started working on it when I got home from college."

"You built this?"

"Every board."

"You must be really good with your hands." She shifted her gaze to meet mine, and her cheeks immediately turned a bright shade of pink. "I mean building stuff."

Fuck me. I'd like to show her exactly how good I could be with my hands. Instead, I hung her coat on the hook next to mine and willed the blood flowing to my cock to divert to other areas of my body. Like my brain, so I could think of something to say that wouldn't sound like a come on. Because coming onto Emma Bradshaw was the only thing I wanted to do.

"Let me get that fire going." I stepped around her to head toward the giant stone fireplace. I'd built it myself using rocks from the riverbed that ran through my property. Focusing on something as mundane as making a fire would give me a chance to get my shit together.

"Can I do anything to help?" She stood behind me.

"Why don't you go grab a pair of sweats and a sweatshirt from the bottom drawer of my dresser," I suggested. That would get her out of my personal space for a few minutes, though I wasn't sure how I'd react to seeing her curves encased by my clothes. "All of my stuff will probably swim on you, but it's better than being all wet."

"You're sure you don't mind?"

All wet... great... now I had visions of her wet and ready for me floating through my head. A strangled "yes" worked its way through my lips. "My bedroom's upstairs."

"Okay." She shuffled to the staircase and made her way to the second floor.

I scooped up the ashes from yesterday's fire while I tried not to picture her rifling through my drawers... touching my things... leaving traces of her scent in the room where I spent most of my time dreaming about her. Dammit. I stacked a few logs on the grate and shoved some pieces of kindling between them.

The fire caught, the flames licking at the newspaper I'd stuffed under the logs. Moose looked up from her fluffy dog bed, a few feet away from where she'd been banished.

"I've got enough going on. I don't need any more crap from you today." At least she'd stayed put after I'd sent her inside.

She looked up at the stairs and let out a soft whine. I followed her gaze to see Emma making her way down the steps. She had on a Mustang Mountain Riders hoodie with the logo emblazoned across her breasts. It looked a hell of a lot better on her than it ever had on me.

"I hope you don't mind, but I borrowed a hairbrush I found in your bathroom drawer." She'd piled her hair up on top of her head, which only made me want to wrap my hand around her exposed neck and kiss the spot where her pulse fluttered.

So much for remaining unaffected. I just needed to keep my distance. Give her space. Distract myself with something else. I took in a long, deep breath and met her at the bottom of the steps. "Give me your wet things and I'll put them in the dryer."

"I can do it if you show me where it is."

"Just hand them over. I'll toss them in on my way to the garage. I need to get out there and shovel if I want to pull my truck in tonight."

She hesitated, then carefully passed me the damp clothes she'd folded into a small pile. "Thank you. Is there anything I can do to help while you're outside?"

"Keep an eye on Moose?"

Hearing her name, Moose lifted her head.

"I can do that. I'll put away the groceries, too."

I'd forgotten the bags I'd set down on the counter. "That would be great. Thanks."

Emma sucked her lower lip into her mouth like she wanted to say something more.

"What is it?" I asked.

"Do you mind if I scrounge around for something to eat? I haven't had anything since I ate half that protein bar for breakfast."

I'd never been accused of being overly hospitable and felt like a complete ass for not asking if she wanted something to eat or drink. "Help yourself to anything you can find. I should have offered before."

She rewarded me with a smile that could have lit up the northern half of Montana. "You've had other things on your mind."

That was an understatement. She had no idea what kind of other things I'd been thinking about, and she never would. "I'll be back in a bit."

I turned to head to the door leading out to the garage. Her clothes slid out of my hand and landed at my feet. I bent down to pick them up and immediately wished I hadn't. A pair of bright blue panties with white snowflakes printed all over them sat half-buried under the long-sleeve shirt she'd had on earlier.

Any hope I had of keeping my mind out of the gutter where Emma was concerned disappeared with a big, fat *poof*.

I DON'T KNOW how I managed to stay on my feet when Jackson bent down to pick up my clothes. Seeing my panties dangling from his thick long fingers almost had me passing out right then and there. It had to have been divine intervention that kept me from making an even bigger fool out of myself than I already had.

He'd disappeared through the doorway to the garage almost a full half hour ago and my hands were still shaking. That made it fairly difficult to dice the onion in front of me, but I kept at it until I'd chopped the entire thing into bits. I hope he liked chicken tortilla soup. It was the only thing I knew how to make from scratch. I usually relied on the internet for recipes, but my phone had no signal.

It might have been because of the heavy snowfall, or maybe my service provider didn't have towers all the way up Mustang Mountain. Either way, I was off the grid. Completely and totally reliant on Jackson for everything. I let out a low groan, wishing I could rely on him in a much different way.

Moose nudged her nose into my hip. After Jackson left, she'd slowly made her way into the kitchen, one cautious step at a time. I'd always loved dogs, though I hadn't lived with one since I moved out of my child-hood home. Back then we had a twenty-five-pound rescue mutt that ruled the roost. I estimated Moose to be at least seventy-five to eighty-five pounds. She and Jackson seemed like a good match. It was nice knowing he had company up here all alone on the mountain.

For a moment, I let myself wonder if he ever had any other female companionship besides his dog. It was none of my business, but I couldn't help the pang of jealousy that sliced through my belly when I pictured some other woman wrapping her arms around Jackson's neck or snuggling into his arms in the king-sized bed I saw in his room.

"Tell me, Moose, does your daddy have a girl-friend?" I tossed her a small piece of cooked chicken. Too bad she couldn't talk. I bet she knew more about Jackson than anyone.

She flicked her tongue out and licked any trace of chicken from her muzzle. Then shifted on her haunches like she was ready for the next treat.

"I don't want to get in trouble for feeding you from the counter."

The onion I'd chopped sizzled in the bottom of a large saucepan. I stirred the pieces with a spatula, then paused to push up my sleeves. Even though Jackson's sweatshirt was several sizes too big, it felt nice and cozy, almost like a hug.

"Your dad's probably a good hugger, isn't he?"

Moose cocked her head.

I wrapped my arms around my middle, pretending they were Jackson's. A comforting masculine scent drifted past my nose. I couldn't describe it. His sweatshirt smelled like a blend of the outdoors. A whiff of pine mingled with something smoky, like the bonfires we used to make on the beach.

"I bet he's good at a lot of things," I mumbled to myself just as the door to the garage opened. Cold air blew in along with Jackson, who looked like he'd lost a snowball fight to the abominable snowman.

"You bet who's good at a lot of things?" He peeled off his coat and hat, then shook the snow from his boots.

"Oh, um, Miles." I glanced over at Moose, who was licking clumps of snow from the floor. "I was just telling your dog that Miles is probably just fine, since he's learned so much from living in Montana."

Jackson's eyes narrowed for a second, then he shot a quick look at the stove. "What smells so good?"

"I threw some soup together. Chicken tortilla. It's the only thing I know how to make without a recipe." My hands twisted together as I blathered. *Stop talking. He's going to think you're an idiot.* "Usually, I look up recipes on my phone, but I don't have a signal here."

"You can log into my wi-fi." Jackson stepped out of his boots and left them on a tray by the door.

"Oh, I didn't think to ask."

He stepped close enough that the chill clinging to him seeped over to me. "Give me your phone and I'll type in the password."

I shivered as I handed over my phone.

"Are you still cold?" His face was windblown and red from being outside for so long.

I reached up and pressed my fingertips to his cheek.

He pulled back like I'd branded him with my touch.

"I'm sorry. I just wanted to see how cold your cheeks were." *Stupid, stupid, stupid.* He obviously didn't want to have anything to do with me.

"Try it now." He pushed my phone into my hands. "I'm going to take a quick shower. You should sit by the fire for a bit to warm up."

"Okay." My pulse whooshed through my ears. I'd never felt so uncomfortable around a man before. Jackson was my brother's best friend. Maybe if I tried to think of him more like a brother, the naughty thoughts I had about him would disappear.

That lasted half a second. Just long enough for him to pull off the long-sleeve flannel shirt he'd been wearing and reveal the clingy tee he had on underneath. The soft white cotton clung to his pecs. I could see the ridges of his abs through the thin fabric.

Forcing myself to turn toward the stove, I reached for the spatula to give the soup another stir. "I'll have this ready by the time you get done."

"Thanks, Em." He took a few steps toward the stairs, then stopped. "It smells really good."

My heart squeezed tight at the compliment. And he'd called me Em. Maybe he didn't hate me. Maybe he just didn't like to be touched. Maybe he was a little irked that he was being forced to invite me into his private space. Whatever the reason, I needed to keep my thoughts and my hands to myself.

FIFTEEN MINUTES LATER, Jackson came down the stairs in a pair of gray sweatpants and a clean t-shirt. His hair was still damp from his shower, but I refused to let myself think about the fact he'd been naked in the same building as me.

"Feel better?" I asked.

"Yeah. Your clothes should be dry by now. After we eat, you're welcome to take a hot shower or soak in my tub. If the snow stops, you can see the stars through the big window in the bathroom. I always thought it would be a good place to relax with a glass of whiskey and... hell, never mind."

"A glass of whiskey and what?" I asked.

"Nothing. How's that soup look?" He pulled two

bowls down from a cabinet and set them on the counter.

"Looks okay, but I don't know how it will taste. I had to make a few substitutions."

He opened a drawer and grabbed a ladle. "You didn't have to make dinner."

"It's not like I had something more important to do."

"I'm not used to people doing things for me," he admitted.

"So, it's okay for you to save me from a wolf, rescue me from being stranded in a blizzard, and bring me back to your place, but you're having a hard time accepting the soup I made with your groceries?" Comparing him to my brother didn't seem like such a stretch. Miles had always been the same way.

"Well, yeah." He shrugged his huge shoulders. "It's just how I'm built."

"I like the way you're built." The words flew out of my mouth before I could stop them.

His head whipped up, and he studied me with eyes the color of the homemade caramels my grandma used to make. I bet he tasted just as sweet. Probably even sweeter.

"I mean, I think that's sweet that you put other people first. It's probably time you let someone take care of you for a bit, though." And holy guacamole, every cell in my body urged me to be that woman. He could obviously handle the day-to-day aspects of his life, but who held him at night? Who gave him a reason to keep putting one foot in front of the other? Who loved him with her whole heart?

"I've been taking care of myself for so long, I wouldn't even know where to start." He carried the two bowls over to the table. "Should we eat?"

I didn't trust myself to say anything else, so I grabbed two spoons and met him at the table. Moose ducked her head and crept close until Jackson snapped his fingers and pointed to where her dog bed sat in front of the glowing fire. She let out a big sigh, then turned circles on top of the bed and finally plopped down. That was exactly how I felt: frustrated and tired. Though I didn't think turning circles and plopping down on the couch would help.

"This is really good." Jackson spooned big bites of chicken and broth into his mouth.

"I'm glad it turned out." I couldn't bring myself to eat. I'd been starving before, but my nerves had taken over. If I added anything to my stomach, I'd probably end up making myself sick.

"Aren't you hungry anymore?"

I shook my head. "Not really. I snacked while I was making dinner. I'm probably just worn out from the drive and everything else that's happened today."

"I'll put some fresh sheets on the bed right after we eat so you can turn in early."

"I'm so tired I could fall asleep here at the table. I can just curl up on the couch. You don't need to give up your bed."

He held the spoon halfway to his mouth. "You're taking the bed."

"Fine. But no clean sheets. I've been enough trouble already." Besides, his sheets probably smelled like him. If I let him switch them out, I'd deprive myself of the ultimate sensory experience.

"Fine."

"Look at that. We just compromised on something." I forced myself to take a couple spoonfuls of soup. If I didn't eat, I was afraid he'd go all bossy grump on me.

"Compromise, hmm. I don't know if that word's ever been part of my vocabulary." His brows arched and I could have sworn his lips tipped up at the corners in an almost smile. "I'll take care of cleaning up if you want to head to bed."

I pushed back from the table. "I'm going to take you up on that."

"Do you need anything? There are extra toothbrushes under the sink upstairs and towels are in the closet in the bathroom. I can come up and set them out for you." He made a move to push back from the table.

"I've got it. I can take care of myself too." With a heaviness in my chest that didn't make sense, I took my dishes over to the sink. The odds of anything happening between us were non-existent. Jackson would never violate the bro code and hook up with his best friend's little sister. Based on how he reacted earlier, he didn't find me attractive at all. Still, there were some wishes a girl just couldn't let go.

I climbed the stairs, fully aware of his gaze on my backside. So what if I added a little extra wiggle to the way my hips shifted from side to side?

"Hey, Emma?" The sound of Jackson's chair scraping on the kitchen floor made me stop.

I gripped the handrail tight as I turned toward him. "Yes?"

"SWEET DREAMS." I stared at her from across the room, willing her to come back to the kitchen and brush her fingers across my cheek like she'd done earlier.

"You too." Her shoulders sagged, then she turned and continued her trek up the stairs. The click of my bedroom door shutting behind her should have provided a sense of closure. Instead, all I could do was stand in the middle of my kitchen and picture her stripping off my sweatshirt and crawling underneath the covers of the bed I wished we'd be sharing.

"Dammit." I set my bowl down on the counter harder than necessary. Moose staggered to her feet. She was used to my grumpy ways but must have sensed my frustration. I bent down to run my hand over her massive head. Maybe I'd spent so much time on my own that I'd lost the ability to effectively communicate with other people. I didn't feel so out of sorts around the guys, though. And I never had any trouble chatting with folks in town, even though I preferred to stay to myself.

Being around Emma had thrown me off. Most of the women I talked to were old enough to be my mother, or in Ruby's case, my grandmother. As I packed up the leftover soup and washed the few dishes we'd dirtied, I tried to remember the last time I'd spoken to a woman close to my age.

Fuck it. I couldn't.

Maybe Ruby was right about the need to attract some new residents to Mustang Mountain. I added another log to the fire before heading into the extra room on the first floor that I used for an office. The other guys needed to know what Ruby was up to. No telling who she might target next. I could handle her and any unwanted attention she sent my way, but some of the other guys might not be as nice about it.

I pulled up my personal email and squinted at the number on the screen. On an average day, I might receive five to ten emails. Most of them were sales pitches from places I shopped online with the occasional check in from a distant family member mixed in. How the hell could I have two hundred-twenty-one unread emails?

Every single one of them had been forwarded from the Mustang Mountain visitor's site. I clicked on the latest.

Dear Jackson,

I was so excited to see your profile on the Mountain Men of Mustang Mountain website. We have so much in common. I also love to cross-country ski and gaze at the stars in a crisp wintry sky. I think I might be the special woman you're looking for. You said you loved kids. I've got three boys and two girls...

I flipped the cover of my laptop closed. The post-cards were one thing but creating a profile and posting it on some website was taking it way too far. It was only a little after seven, but after the day I'd had, I was ready to pour a few fingers of whiskey and zone out in front of the TV for a couple of hours. No doubt I had a long night stretching ahead of me. I probably wouldn't be able to sleep knowing Emma was so close, yet completely out of my reach.

I'd check in with the guys tomorrow. We'd figure out how to put a stop to Ruby's meddling, and I'd get the satellite phone from Ford so I could track down Miles. He needed to come home and find out what had brought Emma to town. In the years Miles had been living in Mustang Mountain, she hadn't visited once. Something must have happened to cause her to drop everything and drive halfway up a mountain in a January blizzard.

Shit. I'd left my phone charging on the bathroom counter when I went up to shower. If I didn't go grab it, my alarm would go off at six and wake her up. The whiskey would have to wait.

Moose got up to follow me, but I signaled for her to stay downstairs. She was used to sleeping at the foot of the bed and probably thought I was trying to leave her behind. Hopeful that Emma hadn't fallen asleep yet and was wearing something that covered every inch of her skin, I swallowed my apprehension and started up the stairs.

I'd just knock on the door and tell her I need to grab my phone. No big deal. Somehow, the closer I got to my own bedroom door, the harder my heart thumped around in my chest.

It was my house. She'd probably expect me to need something from my bedroom before turning in for the night. For fuck's sake, I was almost thirty years old. I could handle myself around a woman. Even a woman as tempting as Emma.

I lifted my fist and landed two soft knocks on the center of the solid wood door. There was no response. I knocked again, a little louder.

Still nothing.

Great.

I wrapped my hand around the doorknob and twisted slowly, hoping she'd be sound asleep. The room was dark. I was usually up before the sun, so I slept with the curtains open, but she must have pulled them closed. The soft sounds of her shallow breath told me she must be sleeping. I shuffled toward the door leading into the bathroom and grabbed my phone from the counter.

Relief coursed through me. I drew in a deep breath

and turned to make my way back through the bedroom when the unmistakable sound of the bedroom door being nudged open hit me. Moose. Dammit. The dog thought it was bedtime and any second, she'd hop onto the bed and try to curl up at Emma's feet.

"Moose, no." I tried to whisper, but since the damn dog barely responded when I yelled at her, I didn't expect her to listen.

The light filtering in from the hall showed Moose preparing to jump. I half ran, half fell toward her, trying to grab her collar before she landed on the bed and scared the crap out of Emma.

I missed.

Moose leapt onto the bed. Emma shot up to a seated position. I landed on my elbow on the hardwood floor.

The lamp on the nightstand turned on, and Emma leaned over the edge of the bed. Her hair fell around her face like a golden halo.

"What are you doing in here?" She struggled to pull the quilt I used as a bedspread out from under Moose, who either didn't realize or didn't care she'd just fucked me over.

I got to my feet and held up my phone. "Sorry. I forgot I left my phone on the bathroom counter, and I didn't want my alarm to go off at six and wake you up."

The deer-in-the-headlights look faded from her eyes. "Thanks, I guess."

"Moose, get off the bed." I glared at my traitorous dog.

"She can stay." Emma gave up on trying to tug the covers and fluffed the pillow instead. "It would be nice to have a warm body to snuggle with."

The hairs on the back of my neck stood on end. "Is that what you're looking for? A warm body to snuggle?"

Her chest rose as she took in a deep breath. I could see her beaded nipples under the fabric of my shirt. My balls tightened. We stared at each other for a painfully long beat.

"Sorry, that was out of line," I said. So out of line. What the fuck was wrong with me? I knew better than to make not-so-thinly veiled passes. Knew better than to make any passes at all, especially at Emma. I rubbed at the back of my neck, wishing I could rewind the past ten minutes or maybe even the whole damn day.

"What are *you* looking for?" She caught me right before I crossed the threshold from the bedroom into the hall.

I whipped around. "What do you mean?"

She held my gaze as she pulled back the covers. "Do you have anything against being a warm body?"

My cock recognized the invitation way before my brain processed her words. Fuck no, I didn't have anything against being the warm body she wanted. "You can't mean it."

"You sure about that?"

I'd never been a man who suffered from a lack of self-control but holding myself back took every bit of restraint I possessed. Hell, I must have channeled some from a parallel universe.

"What about Miles?" I shook my head and wondered if she'd notice me reaching down to adjust the front of my sweats. There was no way to hide what was going on down there. Even the possibility of getting my hands on her had me hard.

"What Miles doesn't know won't hurt him." She slid the covers a little lower. Low enough to show me that she didn't have anything on underneath my over-sized shirt.

"You don't think it will be hard to keep it from him?" I had my doubts, but I wanted to hear it from her. If she wanted me and I wanted her... hell, we were two adults. Two consenting adults.

She glanced at my crotch. "Looks like the only thing hard right now is you."

Dammit, she was impossible to resist. I stalked toward the bed and gestured for Moose to get down. I didn't need any witnesses to what was about to go down with my best friend's little sister.

Emma tugged the covers over her legs. "You just sent my personal heater away."

I closed the door behind the dog. "Don't worry, Em. I'm going to get you so hot, you'll be begging me to open the windows."

"Is that so?"

I nodded, barely able to comprehend what we were about to do. "If we're going to do this, I've got a couple of rules."

"What kind of rules?" She fluttered her lashes.

"Number one. Your brother can never find out about this. No drunken confessions. No guilty admissions. You've got to promise me you'll never tell him."

Her lips tipped up. "Are you afraid of my brother, Jackson?"

"It's a deal breaker."

"Of course, I'll never tell him. Is that it?"

"No." The other rule was trickier. If I let myself have her, it could only be this once. I couldn't continue to be Miles's friend and constantly be wondering what his sister was up to.

"Well?"

"This can only happen once."

Her brows arched, disappearing under the hair falling across her forehead. "As in literally one time or as in just until we aren't stuck inside your cabin together?"

I reached out and brushed her hair away from her face. "I'm not going to be done with you after just one time, Em."

"Any more rules?"

"No, that's it."

She nodded and scooted over to make room for me on the bed. "What are you waiting for then, Jackson?"

I DIDN'T KNOW what had gotten into me to make me so bold, but with Jackson sliding his big body under the covers next to me, it didn't matter. My only concern was how long it would take him to finally kiss me.

He rested on his elbow and leaned over me. The lamp on the nightstand was behind him, but I could still see his eyes darken to a deep shade of brown. He slid his hand up to cup my cheek. Goosebumps pebbled my skin all the way down to my toes. Being this close to him, having him invade my personal space, made me feel like I'd just downed a few glasses of champagne.

He dipped his head toward me and nudged his nose against mine. The scent of his shower gel, something outdoorsy and fresh, filled my nose. I couldn't breathe, couldn't think, couldn't move a muscle. Anticipation temporarily paralyzed me.

Then he slanted his mouth over mine, and our lips

touched. The contact was so brief; I wondered if it actually counted as a kiss. Before I could decide, his mouth was on mine again. This time firm and demanding. Kissing Jackson was everything I'd ever imagined, and so much more. I wanted to stop time, forget about everything else going on, and spend the rest of my life just like this.

His tongue pressed against the seam of my lips. I opened, unable to deny him. The moment his tongue slid next to mine, I knew without a doubt I'd never be the same. I wrapped my arms around his neck and pulled him closer.

Everything else faded away except for the way his mouth felt on mine. Then he slid his hand up my thigh. I squirmed underneath him. A hollow ache pulsed between my thighs. I wanted him. Wanted him like I'd never wanted a man before. Wanted him with a deep need I didn't understand.

"You okay, Em?" His ragged breath matched mine.

"More than okay."

His thumb swept along my jawbone and his eyes softened at the edges. "I'm going to ask you one last time. Are you sure this is what you want?"

I studied him... the concerned crease of his brow, the question in his eyes.

"More than anything." It was the truth. I'd dreamed about this for so long. Now that we'd finally crossed the line, every part of me burned for him.

"Good." He reached behind his neck and pulled

his t-shirt over his head. I stared at his chiseled pecs. His body looked too perfect to touch.

I ran my hands over his shoulders, up the back of his neck, and cupped his cheeks between my palms. His eyes closed, and he lowered his head to kiss my neck. My pulse jumped. A shiver raced down my spine. In all the times I'd fantasized about Jackson, it had never felt this good. I wanted to memorize everything about this moment so I could relive it over and over and over again.

His kisses trailed over my collarbone. I wished I'd grabbed my dry clothes and put on my bra and panties. With no barrier between my skin and the shirt I'd borrowed from him, my nipples scraped against the cotton. He sucked one into his mouth through the front of the shirt. I let out a gasp, totally unprepared for the rush of heat that hurtled through my veins.

He continued kissing his way down my stomach. His hands eased the hem of the shirt up. I wasn't ready for him to see me, to feel the extra padding around my thighs and belly.

"What's wrong?" He lifted his head. "Do you want me to stop?"

"No, it's just... maybe we could turn out the light?"

Jackson's eyes narrowed. "Why would I do that? Then I wouldn't be able to see you, beautiful."

I rolled my head, glancing at the lamp. "That's kind of my point."

"Em,"—He reached up and turned my head to

meet his gaze—"you're perfect. I've been fantasizing about this for years."

The truth in his eyes melted any resistance. "Okay."

He grinned, then slid the shirt up my thighs, past my hips, until his lips brushed my bare skin. I was going to come, and he hadn't even touched me below the waist. My breath caught in my throat, and I tried to stop the wave of pleasure threatening to pull me under.

Jackson lifted his head. "Don't you dare come yet, Em. Not until I've tasted you."

I grabbed fistfuls of the sheets as I tried to hold back. My muscles tightened, every part of me taut with the effort of not giving in.

Then Jackson licked his lips. "This is going to be fun."

The sight of his mouth so close to my throbbing, aching pussy pushed me so close to the edge. He nudged my legs apart, spreading me wide. Then lowered his head and sucked my clit into his mouth.

Fireworks exploded behind my eyelids. My release slammed into me. I bit down on my lip to try to keep from crying out. It didn't work. My hips bucked, and I ground my pussy against him. His rough whiskers scraped the inside of my thighs, but I didn't care. Didn't care about anything except what Jackson was doing between my legs.

He didn't let up until my legs gave out and I collapsed back on the bed. Then he reached into the drawer of his nightstand, and I watched him strip off his pants and wrap his hand around his giant cock. He stroked himself from base to tip a couple of times. I wanted to reach out and run my finger down his length, but my body was still boneless from the mind-blowing orgasm he'd just delivered.

"Are you ready for me, Em?"

"I'm not sure I can move yet," I admitted. As much as I wanted to pull him onto me and wrap my legs around his waist, aftershocks still rushed through me.

"It's okay, angel. I'll do all the work." He rolled the condom down his length and hovered over me, his thick cock nudging into my thigh.

Then he eased into me, taking his time, letting me stretch to accommodate him. The hollow ache I'd felt before gave way to the fullness I'd craved.

"You feel so good." His breath brushed my ear.

"So good," I agreed as I clenched around him.

He increased the pace, pulling almost all the way out before thrusting deep inside me. The same pressure I'd felt before started to build again, this time stronger.

I dug my nails into his shoulders, encouraging him to keep going. His hips pistoned back and forth. I was close to coming again when he reached down and fingered my clit. He knew how to coax sensations from me that I'd never even imagined. Each time he seated himself all the way inside me, he sent me flying higher. Higher and higher until there was nowhere else to go.

That's when I exploded around him.

Jackson

THE LITTLE NOISES coming from the back of her throat spurred me on. She was on the edge again, and I'd do anything to send her flying over.

"That's it, Em. Come for me, angel." I gave her clit a gentle pinch and felt the walls of her pussy clench around my cock. The glazed look in her eyes made my heart swell. I stopped holding back, so desperate to join her. A few more thrusts and I was there. My balls tightened, then I pumped my release into her, giving her everything I had. At that moment, I wished there wasn't a fucking condom between us. I wanted to fill her with my seed and put a baby in her belly that would tie us together forever.

Spent, I collapsed on top of her, being careful not to crush her under my weight. I pressed gentle kisses against her cheeks, her eyelids, her forehead. I never wanted to stop kissing her. Never wanted to stop touching her or feeling her soft skin underneath me.

She lightly raked her nails down my back. If I'd died right then, I'd die a happy man. But I couldn't die yet. I still had several precious hours to spend with Emma before reality would crash in, and the bubble we'd created around ourselves would burst.

I shifted, rolling over to the other side of the bed so

I could get up and take care of the condom. "Be right back."

She mumbled something I couldn't make out. Traveling all day had to have been exhausting. She needed sleep more than I needed to be back inside her. I could wait. Emma's needs came first. I'd never felt the urge to take care of someone like I wanted to care for her. I'd be lying to myself if I tried to downplay the depth of the feelings I had for her.

No matter what happened, this thing between us couldn't last. We both knew that going in. The rules hadn't changed. But if I was being honest with myself, I knew the first time I touched her that a lifetime with her would never be enough. How could I expect to be happy with just the sliver of time we'd carved out for ourselves for a secret one-night fling?

By the time I got back to the bed, she was sound asleep. Her golden hair fanned out on the pillow around her, and she had the covers pulled all the way up to her chin. I slid into the bed behind her, curled my body around hers, and tried to pretend we had all the time in the world.

Even though I'd never felt more content, sleep wouldn't come. That was okay, though. I didn't want to waste a single second on sleep when I could be watching Emma. I tried to memorize the way the soft lamplight brought out the deep gold highlights in her hair. My lungs filled with the scent of her shampoo. It smelled like piña coladas and made me picture the two of us splashing in the surf on some deserted island.

She was everything I'd ever wanted in a woman, yet we could never be together. Still, she was mine. I knew it deep down in my soul. She was made for me, and I'd be hers forever.

The cry of a lone wolf rang out in the stillness of the night. It hung on the wind, a plaintive anthem. I'd always been content alone. Feeling Emma's touch made me wonder if I'd been lying to myself. Also made me wonder how I was supposed to let her go when our time together came to an end.

I OPENED my eyes and looked around the unfamiliar room. Flashes from the night before played through my head. Had I really propositioned Jackson Hill?

The way his arm draped over my waist and the warmth of his big body curled around me proved last night hadn't been a dream. *Thank you, past self, for having the guts to make a move.* I rubbed my thighs together and remembered how it felt to have his beard scrape against my skin.

A shiver raced down my spine. I rolled over so I could study Jackson while he was lost to sleep.

Lashes that were far too thick and long to belong to a man fanned over his cheeks. In the soft morning light filtering through a slit in the curtains, I could see the faint remainder of a scar above one eyebrow. His full lips begged to be kissed, even in slumber.

I'd agreed to his rules because that was the only

way he'd take me, but now that we'd spent one night together, I wished things could be different.

A scratching noise came from the door. Poor Moose. She'd been kicked off the bed last night. Reluctantly, I rolled out of bed so I could go let her out. I found a thick, warm robe hanging on the back of the bathroom door and shoved my feet into a pair of way-too-big-for-me slippers by the foot of the bed.

Moose rushed down the stairs ahead of me and went straight to the back door. It was barely after six and the sun hadn't even started to rise. I had no idea what Jackson did for a living, but a quick glance out the back door showed the snow had continued to fall overnight. Would he really be able to get us back down the mountain?

The selfish part of me that wanted to think of him as mine hoped we'd have another day together. It didn't seem like too much to ask, especially since we'd both agreed we could never get together again. I'd have to be happy taking what I could. My brother had never had an easy time making friends. It would be cruel to make Jackson choose between his friendship with Miles or me. Not to mention how devastated I'd be when he didn't pick me.

I waited by the back door while the big dog leapt through the snow. She did her business, then reappeared on the deck, her body covered in white.

"Get in here. It's too cold to be outside." I brushed the snow off her back before it fell all over the gorgeous wood floors.

As long as I was up, I figured I might as well make coffee. I hadn't eaten too much last night and my stomach rumbled. After a quick search through the cabinets for coffee, I had a pot brewing. Figuring I could scramble some eggs and serve Jackson breakfast in bed, I had my nose stuck in the refrigerator when I heard his footsteps coming down the stairs.

"What are you doing up so early?" He came up behind me and nudged his hips into my backside.

The feel of something long and hard against my ass sent a rush of heat across my cheeks. I'd been worried he'd think last night was a mistake. "Your dog needed to go out."

"She probably just wanted your attention." Jackson spun me around slowly and backed me up against the door to the fridge. "Too bad I'm not willing to share you with anyone."

"Is that so?"

His hand parted the front of the robe and slid down my belly. I shivered, but not from being cold.

"Yeah, that's so. There's no way either one of us is going anywhere today. That means you're mine for another twenty-four hours." He dipped his head and kissed a spot behind my ear that had to be one of the most erogenous zones on my body. My nipples immediately beaded. I silently wished for him to hoist me onto the granite counter and have his way with me right next to his Mr. Coffee.

"Don't you want breakfast first?"

He pulled away and slid a hand up the back of my neck. "All I want to eat this morning is you, Em."

Heat pooled low in my belly. "You can't say things like that."

"Why not?" His forehead touched mine and his eyes drilled into mine. "Does it bother you how much I want you?"

"Bother me?" I sputtered out the words. "No, it doesn't bother me at all. It turns me on."

"Let me check." He crowded me against the door, his hands skimming over my hips. One finger dipped down between my curls and parted my folds. "Mmm, yeah, you're turned on all right."

"What are you going to do about it?"

He swept me up in his arms and carried me toward the stairs.

"Put me down before you hurt yourself." I was proud of my curves, but I didn't want him to throw out his back. That would put a quick and disappointing end to the short time we had together.

"I haul logs bigger than you for fun, angel." He kissed the tip of my nose. "Now, be a good girl and hold on tight. I don't want you to bump your head on the way up."

Good girl. My heart melted. I *so* wanted to be his good girl. I wrapped my arms around his neck and held on tight. We got to the top of the steps and Jackson took me back into the bedroom. He kicked the door shut behind us to keep the dog out, then crawled onto the bed with me still in his arms.

"Any regrets about what happened last night?" The sincerity in his eyes caught me off guard.

I shook my head. He didn't act like he thought it was a mistake, but since he brought it up, I needed to know for sure. "Do you regret it?"

"No. The only regret I have is that I only got to be inside you once." He reached into the nightstand to grab another condom. "If you're up for it, I'd like to take care of that right now."

"If I'm up for it?" I slid my gaze to the tented front of his snug gray sweatpants. "Sure looks like you are."

He chuckled. I liked this flirty side of Jackson. It was one I'd never seen before. One I bet he didn't let very many people see.

"I can't be held responsible for the way my body reacts to you." His hand slid under the robe again and clamped onto my hip. "You make me want things I shouldn't, Em."

"Like what?" I needed to know.

"You, angel." He pulled the tie of the robe loose and rolled me onto his chest. "I want all of you."

"You've got me." At least until we left his cabin. I straddled his hips, eager to grind against the thick, growing bulge.

He slid his pants over his hips and ripped open the condom wrapper. "This is the last one I've got, so we'd better make it count."

"Challenge accepted." I let the robe fall away from my shoulders while he unrolled the condom down his length. Then I spread my legs and slid down onto his cock. The pressure gave way to the same fullness I'd felt the night before.

"That's it. Ride me how you need to, Em. I want to watch you take what you want from me, angel."

Hesitant, I reached for the rustic wooden headboard and wrapped my fingers around the wide log running along the top. Lifting my hips, I clenched the walls of my pussy as I slowly raised my hips. Jackson's hands loosely held my waist.

"You're so fucking beautiful like this." He lifted his hips as I lowered mine. Our bodies slapped together. He trailed his fingers from my hip to cup one of my breasts. "So gorgeous."

"Keep talking," I mumbled. The rough edges of his voice made me wild, ripped away any inhibitions holding me back.

"You like it when I talk dirty to you?"

I bit down on my bottom lip and nodded as I sank back onto his cock.

He cupped both of my breasts in his hands and brushed his thumbs over my tight, aching nipples. "I need you, Em. Need to feel you riding my cock. Need to see the look in your eyes when you come. Your pussy is mine, you understand?"

"Yes." I sighed, ready to give myself over to the pressure building inside.

"All mine. And I'm going to take you how I need you."

"Yes, please." My grip on the headboard tightened. It bounced against the wall.

He pinched one nipple, then sat up and sucked the other into his mouth. His teeth scraped over my sensitive skin as he swirled his tongue around the hardened bud. I couldn't stop, didn't want to stop, didn't want the moment to end. I kept one hand on the headboard and funneled the other through his hair, holding him against me.

My orgasm ripped through me. I slowed the pace, wanting to savor the sensations rolling over me.

"That's it. Now look at me," Jackson commanded.

I gazed down at him as I slid up and down his cock. His lips spread into a gorgeous smile. This was what I wanted. This was what I dreamed about when I pictured the kind of life I needed.

Jackson held me close until I sank down on him and wrapped my arms around his shoulders. I couldn't support my own weight, not when every muscle in my body had been wrung out from my release.

"Can you handle a little more, angel?"

"Yes." I could always handle more of him. However he wanted me, I'd let him have me.

"Come here." He gently rolled me onto my stomach. "Think you can get up on your knees for me?"

I pushed myself up on all fours, more than willing to have him take me from behind.

Jackson ran his hand down my back, his fingers trailing over each individual vertebra. When he reached my ass, he clamped his hands to my hips and lined himself up to enter me from behind. I was still soaked from my own release, so he slid in easily.

"I can't tell you how many times I've dreamed about having you like this." He pushed into me.

At this angle, everything felt different, but my body still buzzed with pleasure. Knowing he'd thought about me the same way I'd thought about him made our joining so bittersweet. At least we had this time together. I wouldn't let myself think about any of this coming to an end. Not now. Not while he was moving inside me, filling me with his cock, making me feel more cherished than I ever had before in my life.

THE STORM finally let up right before dark. By that time, I'd explored every inch of Emma's body with my hands, my lips, and my tongue. The woman fascinated me. She was so open, so willing to give me everything I needed from her. Tomorrow we'd have to face reality. I'd put off meeting with the guys because of the storm, but we were supposed to get together around lunchtime at the diner in town. Ford was bringing the satellite phone and by nightfall tomorrow, Miles would be back, and Emma wouldn't have a reason to spend another night with me.

I already missed her, even though I had my arms curled around her. She leaned against me while she ran a hand over Moose, who was snuggled up next to us on the couch. We were watching some rom-com, but the only thing I was paying attention to was Emma.

"If you're not into the movie, we can turn it off," she said.

"I'm just more into you than what's happening on TV." I gave her a squeeze and kissed the top of her head.

She turned to look up at me. "Do you want to talk about tomorrow?"

Hell no, I didn't want to talk about tomorrow. I wasn't ready to think about how I'd feel when she left for good. "Not really."

"How mad do you think Miles would be if we told him about us?"

"Told him what? That I seduced his baby sister and spent the last twenty-four hours with my cock buried inside her?" My gut twisted with guilt. "I think he'd be pretty damn mad."

"You're right." She faced forward.

As much as I wanted to hold on to her, I couldn't betray my friendship with her brother. Miles had a reason to be guarded. He'd gone through a rough break up during college that made him question everything. His ex not only cheated on him repeatedly, but she made him think he was nuts for even suspecting it. She'd done a real number on him and when he finally realized what was happening, he cut her out of his life for good. If I told him I'd gone behind his back and messed around with Emma, he'd never forgive me. And I couldn't afford to be the reason for creating a rift between the group of guys I considered family.

"I wish things were different," I admitted.

"No use wasting a wish on something that can never be. It's all for the best, though." She flipped the television off and pushed up from the couch. "I think I'm going to turn in. Do you want to join me, or should we end things now?"

I squinted up at her, trying to get a read on what she wasn't saying. I'd never be ready to let her go, but her needs came first. "What do you want to do?"

"Honestly?"

Nodding, I set my hands on her waist. "I always want you to be honest with me, angel."

"You'd better stop calling me that. I'd hate for it to slip out in front of my brother." Her shoulders rose and fell as she took in a deep breath.

"Emma, what's wrong?" A part of her had shut down. I felt it like she'd slammed a door in my face. She'd been so open, so warm and willing, and now the tension between us was icy cold.

"I'm fine. It's just... I came all the way up here because I got laid off at work." She broke eye contact. "I know how much Miles loves it here and thought I might like it too."

"Do you like it here?" A heavy weight thudded to the bottom of my gut. I thought she might stay for a day or two max, then head back to California. Though it wouldn't be easy to forget her, knowing she was so far away might make it bearable. But if she stayed in Mustang Mountain... how would I be able to handle her being so close and so out of my reach?

"I love it here. The town is right out of a Hallmark movie. I'd probably need some lessons on how to drive in the snow, but I think it's beautiful." She met my gaze briefly, then looked away again. "I thought Miles might let me stay with him for a little while and help me find a job. Otherwise, it looks like I'll have to move back in with my parents."

"Whatever you want to do, we can make it work." A war raged inside me. Would it be better to be able to see her in town but know she'd never be mine or never see her again? I didn't know the answer. But whatever Emma wanted, I'd do my best to make it happen for her.

"How?" Her eyes had a glassy shine to them, like she was about to cry. I wouldn't be able to handle that. I'd once dislocated my own shoulder to get out of a crack between the rocks I'd fallen into, but I wasn't strong enough to see the woman I loved cry. Fuck, when did the "L" word enter my mind?

"I don't know yet, but I want you to be happy. If that means you stay in Mustang Mountain and we keep the past few days a secret, that's fine. I do most of my work from here, so there's not much of a chance of us running into each other in town." I wouldn't be able to look forward to Ruby's coffee anymore. Though if she continued to plaster my picture and profile all over the internet to entice random single women to come to town, I'd be avoiding Nelson's anyway.

"Mustang Mountain belongs to you."

"The mountain doesn't belong to anyone. That's the beauty of this place. It's wild and rugged and can't be controlled by anyone or anything." Kind of like my feelings for Emma, I realized. I couldn't wish them away. Couldn't stop them from growing any more than I'd be able to stop the bitterroot flowers from spreading up the hillsides in springtime.

"You think we could co-exist here?" She turned her gaze on me again. The hope in her blue eyes turned them the color of a bright summer Montana sky.

"If that's what you want, I'll make it happen." I'd do anything for her, even try to live within the walls of an invisible prison. That's what it would feel like having her so close and so far beyond my reach.

"Thanks, Jackson." She held out her arms, and I stood to pull her into a hug. Even if she couldn't be mine, I'd be able to keep an eye on her and make sure she stayed safe. Miles would expect the guys in the club to look out for his baby sister. He'd also expect us to treat her like family, which meant no one else would touch her. That should have provided a sense of peace, but it didn't.

We had one last night. At least we could spend it together. "Do you still want to head to bed?"

"I do."

"You go on up. I'll let Moose out and be right behind you." It had been at least an hour since I'd had her. Knowing this would be the last time, I planned on savoring it. I might not be the man she'd spend the rest of her life with, but I wanted to make sure she'd never forget our time together.

I stared out at a full moon while I waited for Moose to come back inside. January's full moon was also called the Wolf Moon. My grandmother always put more faith in the ways of the old world than the new. I remembered her telling me how to harness the energy of the Wolf Moon and that it was a time to trust my instincts and listen to my inner wisdom. I wished she were still alive. Maybe then I could ask her where my inner wisdom had gone. Obviously, it had failed me when I decided to take Emma Bradshaw into my bed.

With a heavy heart, I climbed the stairs to spend one last night with the woman who'd reminded me what it felt like to be a man.

I STRETCHED, opening my eyes to find the bright morning sun shining through the shades. Jackson must have opened them. My heart swelled as I turned, expecting to find him sound asleep next to me.

He was gone.

Moose curled up at my feet. She lifted her head, then set it back down again.

I got up, hoping he was in the bathroom or maybe downstairs getting the coffee going. Last night I'd admitted I wanted to stay in Mustang Mountain. What I hadn't told him was that I planned on coming clean with my brother. I'd never be able to live so close to Jackson and pretend I didn't have feelings for him. Not when my heart had become full the moment his lips touched mine.

Miles would be mad, but we'd weather that storm together. All I wanted for my brother was for him to find happiness... the kind of happiness I'd found with

Jackson. We'd make him understand. He had to because I wasn't prepared to give up until he did.

I pulled on Jackson's robe and headed down the stairs, expecting to see him barefoot and bare chested in front of the kitchen counter. He'd left half a pot of coffee in the carafe, but it was barely warm. That meant he had to have left hours ago. I shuffled in his too big slippers across the front room. Jackson wasn't in his office, so I checked the garage. It wasn't until I shut the door behind me and turned to head back into the kitchen that I saw the note he'd left on the counter. With shaky hands, I picked it up and read over the words he'd scrawled.

Angel,

Thank you for the past couple of days. Being with you was everything I ever dreamed it could be and more. I went into town to pick up the satellite phone so I can call your brother. Assuming I can reach him, he should be back before nightfall. I'll ask him to stop by so you can follow him back to his cabin. I plowed the road so you shouldn't have any trouble with moving snowbanks. I think it would be best if we didn't see each other today, so I'll plan on staying away until you're gone.
I wish things could be different, but I can't hurt your brother.

You'll always have my heart,
Jackson

THE NOTE FELL AWAY as I lifted my hands to cover my face. He didn't want me. I'd shared pieces of my heart with him that I'd never opened to anyone, and he wanted me to leave.

I wasn't going to sit in his cabin with reminders of him surrounding me while I waited hours for Miles to make his way down the mountain. Screw that. I stumbled up the stairs and changed back into the clothes I'd been wearing the day Jackson found me. Even though it had stopped snowing, if I wanted to get back to my car, I'd have quite a way to go in the bitter cold. I rummaged around until I found a pair of snow pants and a beat-up pair of old boots in the bottom of a closet.

I didn't want to take anything of Jackson's with me, but I also didn't want to freeze to death. Once I reached my car, I could leave his stuff on the porch at my brother's cabin. Moose lifted her head and whined.

"I'm sorry, girl. Take good care of him, will you?"

She cocked her head. Then her long pink tongue swept over my hand.

"I'll miss you, too." Tears welled, but I ignored them. I took one last look at the bed where we'd spent so much of the past two nights. Then I turned my back and prepared myself for the long walk back to my car.

The woods were quiet on the way down the mountain. With the sun bright above, the cold didn't bother me nearly as much as I thought it would. It helped that I'd bundle myself up in Jackson's gear. It swam on me, but I didn't care what I looked like. There was no one up here to see me.

If my heart hadn't just been broken, I might have appreciated the beauty of the woods. Tall pines stretched toward the sky, their branches laden with the freshly fallen snow. Birds chirped from the treetops. I even saw tracks through the snow. Thanks to the quick lesson he'd given me the other day when we let Moose out, I was able to pick out deer and a couple of rabbits. A set of larger prints looked like they might belong to a dog, or maybe even the wolf I'd heard howling the past two nights.

By the time I reached my SUV, I could barely feel my toes. Jackson had cleared the snow from around the bumper. I'd been a little worried it wouldn't start, but the engine caught right away. I let it warm up while I stripped off the boots, snow pants, gloves, and coat I'd borrowed and set them on the front porch.

After reading that note, I knew I couldn't stay in Mustang Mountain. As much as I wanted to see Miles, I was barely holding myself together. He'd know as soon as he looked at me that something happened. I could try to lie, but I was afraid I'd end up coming clean and ruining his friendship with Jackson. It was easier if I left. I'd call him when I got back to San Diego.

With a final look at the cabin where I'd hoped to find a new life, I turned the SUV around in the space Jackson had cleared and headed down the mountain.

Jackson

I SAT at the big table against the back wall at the diner and wished I was still curled around Emma's warm body. Sleep hadn't come last night, and I'd spent hours holding her in my arms, listening to the soft sounds she made and hoping she was dreaming of me.

"What the fuck, Jackson?" Mack set his mug of coffee down hard on the table. "Where the hell are you?"

I shook my head, trying to dislodge memories of my time with Emma. "Sorry, man. What were you saying?"

He rolled his eyes and a few of the other guys grumbled. "You're the one who called this meeting. What are we all doing here?"

I pulled the postcard out of my back pocket and unfolded it on the table. "It's Ruby. Did you see this?"

Ford reached for it first. "She talked you into showing off a little skin, huh?"

"She didn't talk me into anything." I ripped the postcard away from him. "She must have taken a picture when I stopped to chop some wood for her and Orville. Now she's got my picture plastered all over the internet and created some website where she posted a dating profile."

Mack bit back a smile. "I didn't know you were on the market."

"I'm not." I could handle a little good-natured ribbing from the guys, but the sidelong looks some of the other town residents were sending my way unnerved me. "She thinks all of us need to settle down and attract more families to town before we end up like Wolf Canyon."

"She's not wrong." Ford leaned back in his chair. "I wouldn't mind having more kids Izzy's age around."

I admired him for single-handedly raising his five-year-old daughter but wasn't ready to be the guinea pig for Ruby's matchmaking endeavors. "Let Ruby fix you up then."

He elbowed me in the ribs. "Screw that."

"She started with me, but I'm sure she's got plans for all of us. If you don't want your picture plastered across her new website, we've got to work together to stop her."

"She can put my picture up. I'll scare all the eligible women away for y'all," Mack offered. He might joke about his scars, but we all knew how much they bothered him.

I was about to tell him to shut the fuck up. Any woman who couldn't look past the suffering he'd endured wouldn't deserve him. My phone rang with Miles's number. I'd managed to reach him earlier with the satellite phone Ford brought, and he said he'd call when he got close enough to pick up cell service.

My gut twisted with guilt as I reached for my phone. "Hey, you back?"

"Yeah. Just pulled up to your place. Where's my sister?"

Panic sent my pulse skyrocketing, and I shifted forward in my seat. "What do you mean? I left her at my cabin to wait for you."

Miles let out a huff. "She's not here. The front door was unlocked, so I went inside and looked around. There's no sign of her."

I got up so quickly that my chair crashed to the linoleum floor behind me. "What do you mean, she's not there? Where the hell could she have gone?"

"I don't know. I'm going to head back to my place. Maybe she's there."

"How would she get back to your cabin? She didn't have a vehicle... unless..." My cheeks went numb.

"Unless what?"

"You don't think she would have tried to walk, do you?"

"Why would she try to walk down the mountain when she knew I was coming for her?" The sound of his engine catching came through the phone.

I'd scared her away. I knew it deep down in my heart. If anything happened to her, I wouldn't be able to live with myself.

"Jackson?" Miles barked. "What happened between you and my sister?"

"Give me a few minutes to finish up in town, and I'll meet you at your place."

"Don't bother. You stay put. I'm heading over to my cabin, and I'll call you when I find out whether she's there." The tone in his voice meant he didn't want to be challenged.

"Okay. I'm at the diner. I'll wait for you here."

He hung up without saying anything else. A big ball of dread lodged in my throat.

"You, okay?" Ford got up to set my chair upright.

"Yeah." I sat down and scooted close to the table. No sense telling the guys what kind of trouble I'd caused with Emma. They'd find out soon enough, and I didn't want to distract them from the goal of stopping Ruby before she caused any more issues.

Asher leaned an elbow on the table. "Did Miles catch anything good up at Lake Bliss?"

Worry for Emma drove every other thought out of my head. I glanced up at Asher. "He didn't say. You'll have to ask him yourself next time you see him."

"Is he coming here?" Mack asked. "I need to get back up to my place to get through evening chores."

"I've got to go pick up Izzy from her after-school program." Ford slid out from the table. "Why don't we all take a few days to think about how we want to handle Ruby? We can talk about it when we get together again."

"Yeah, that's fine." I lifted my hand in a slight wave as Ford and Mack got up from the table.

"Until then, you might want to keep your pretty face out of the limelight." Mack landed a playful punch to my shoulder.

I managed a half-hearted laugh, but thoughts of Ruby's scheme were far from my mind. All I could think about was Emma. Emma stranded in another snowbank. Emma slipping on her walk from my place to her brothers and lying hurt in the woods. Just let her be okay.

The other guys got up and left, but I didn't dare move until Miles called. While I waited, Ruby and Orville entered the diner. My hackles rose, ready for a confrontation.

They sat down at a table a few feet away. Orville lifted his hand in a friendly wave. His wife must not have filled him in on what she'd been up to.

"Hey, Jackson. Care to join us for an early dinner?" Orville offered a grin and gestured toward the empty spot between them.

"Don't mind if I do." I got up and pulled my chair over to their table for two. "What have both of you been up to recently?"

"The usual," Orville said. "Work at the mercantile has been keeping us busy. We just finished our year-end inventory. I think I'm getting too old to climb around the storeroom and count canned goods."

"It's too bad we don't have any younger folks moving into town. I bet you could use some help at the merc." I glared at Ruby as I spoke.

She ignored me and reached out to cover Orville's hand. "We get by, don't we, dear?"

"We sure do. I'd be lost without this woman by my side." The look he gave her reeked of the kind of love that had stood the test of time during their forty-year-plus marriage.

Ruby held her chin high and turned to me. "That's what I want for all of you boys. For you to find the kind of love I have with my Orville."

My chest squeezed the walls of my heart so tight I could barely force a breath through. "And you think posting fake dating profiles to some mountain man website is the best way to go about that?"

Orville's forehead wrinkled and Ruby's lips pursed. "I'm just trying to help. Did you see any of the emails from those women?"

"No, I deleted them all. I don't need help finding the love of my life."

"Well, you sure don't seem to be looking very hard on your own." She crossed her arms over her chest.

Orville looked from me to his wife. "What did you do, love?"

My phone rang. I punched the button and held it to my ear. "Did you find her?"

I GRIPPED the steering wheel so tight my fingers ached as I navigated the big SUV down the mountain. I'd barely spent any time in Mustang Mountain, but I felt like I was leaving home. That was ridiculous since I'd been born and raised outside San Diego and never lived anywhere else. Why did it feel like I was leaving everything important behind when I passed the sign thanking me for visiting Mustang Mountain?

The drive to Kalispell took less than an hour. I hadn't booked a return flight since I'd hoped to be spending some time at Miles's place. Buying a last-minute ticket home would cost me a small fortune, but I couldn't stay. Jackson wasn't willing to fight for me. I couldn't bear to be around him, knowing that what we had wasn't important enough for him to see it through.

I didn't know what I'd do when I got home. Pack up my apartment and move back in with Mom and

I had my suitcase back. There wasn't anything important inside, but I didn't want to leave anything behind. I had no plans to ever return to Mustang Mountain.

Once I'd turned in my rental and maxed out my credit card by buying one of the last tickets on the flight, I sat down to wait. The sun that had been shining so brightly earlier had disappeared behind a wall of clouds. The weather report called for another winter storm. Hopefully, I'd be long gone before that hit.

Finally, it was my turn to board the plane. I took my window seat and shoved my earbuds into my ears to prevent anyone from trying to make pointless conversation. Then I closed my eyes and hoped with all my heart by the time I landed in San Diego, I'd forget all about Jackson Hill.

After a two-hour layover in Salt Lake City, the plane touched down at the San Diego International Airport. I gathered my bag and made it all the way to where I'd parked in long-term parking before I remembered to turn on my phone.

There were three messages from Miles and several texts. It was after eleven, but no doubt Miles wouldn't go to bed until he heard my voice. I got in the car and took a few deep, long breaths before I pushed the button to connect us through my car.

"Where the hell are you, Emma? I've been calling for hours." He sounded tired and pissed. So pissed.

I cleared my throat and forced my voice to go up an octave. "Happy belated birthday. I came in to surprise you, but had to get home for work. I left you a note. Didn't you see it?"

"Cut the crap. Jackson told me you got laid off."

"He did?" Great. What else did he tell my brother?

"Yeah. Said you mentioned looking for a job around Mustang Mountain. Why didn't you wait around for me to come back? You know I'll help you however I can." His voice softened. At least he wasn't yelling at me anymore, but the care and concern in his tone was worse.

"I need to figure out what's best. You know me, I'm too spontaneous. Hopping on a plane and heading your way was a knee-jerk reaction to losing my job. I need some time to decide what I want to do." The lies rolled off my tongue way too easily. I knew exactly what I wanted; I just couldn't have it.

"You could have stuck around a few days. We haven't seen each other in over a year. Why the rush to get home if you don't have a job to get back to?"

"I didn't want to put you out." Or run into your best friend who I happened to fall in love with while I was there.

"You're my sister. You'd never be putting me out."

"Good to know. Maybe I'll come back and visit once I get moved back in with Mom and Dad." I couldn't keep up my end of the conversation much longer. Not when tears threatened. "Hey, I'm about to pull onto the highway, so I'm going to let you go. I'll call you in a few days when I figure out what I want to do, okay?"

"You sure you don't want to come back?"

"I'm sure. Take care of yourself. Now that I've been there, I can see why you love it so much. Bye, Miles." I ended the call before I completely fell apart.

Jackson

"SO, she's back in San Diego already?" I sat on Miles's couch, in the same spot where I'd spent the past six hours. Until I knew Emma was safe, I'd been useless.

"Sounds like it." He set the phone down on the couch cushion. "It just doesn't make sense. Why would she come all this way then leave before I even had a chance to see her?"

I stood and sucked in a deep breath. "There's something I need to tell you."

"Is this about that flyer Ruby put up all over town? I saw a couple of them up at the lodge by Lake Bliss when I stopped in." He leaned forward and rested his forearms on his thighs. "I didn't realize you were so hard up for female companionship."

There wasn't going to be an easy way to tell him. Better to get it over with so we could move past it. "Emma left because of me."

"What?" Miles looked up at me, his brow creased. "Were you an asshole to her?"

"Yeah, but not in the way you probably think."

"What did you say to my sister?" He got to his feet and got right in my face.

He had every right to be pissed, and I'd let him take out his anger on me however he saw fit. "It's more what I didn't say, I think."

"Well, you'd better say something before I beat the shit out of you."

"I like her." Though I'd rather stab my eyes out with a hot poker, I held his gaze.

A muscle ticked along his jaw. "What the fuck did you just say?"

"I like her a lot. I was just too stupid to tell her while she was here."

"I don't get it. Did something happen between the two of you?" His hands clenched into fists. "Did you— fuck, I can't even say it—did you hook up with Emma?"

"Yes, and I know you want to kick my ass and I'll be more than happy to let you, but can I finish talking first?" Miles and I were about the same size, but he had the advantage of anger and adrenaline buzzing through his veins. Before he swung the first punch, I wanted him to know exactly what Emma meant to me.

"You'd better talk fast." He lowered his hands to his sides, but I could feel his rage rolling off him.

"I didn't plan on falling for her. You know I'd never do anything to hurt you. You're like a brother to me."

"Which means you ought to be thinking about Emma like a sister, you asshole. Not taking advantage of her while I was gone." Hate shone from his eyes.

"It wasn't like that." I didn't know how to make

him understand. Funneling my hands through my hair, I tried to find a way to convey the depth of my feelings. "I love her, okay?"

"No, it's not okay." His first punch landed against my jaw. Every part of me urged me to fight back, but I deserved every bit of damage he wanted to inflict.

I staggered backwards, stunned at the sharp pain radiating out from where his fist had connected. It surprised me I could still feel anything besides the numbness that had filled me since Emma left.

"You can't love her. She deserves more than what you'll ever be able to give her."

"You're right. I wish it worked that way, but I can't help the way I feel. Now that I know where she is, I'm going to go after her and tell her."

"No. Leave her alone." Miles shook out his hand.

"I can't. She needs to know. If she sends me away, I'll leave." It would kill me, but I'd honor her wishes. "I don't expect you to understand or forgive me. She's the one. I've spent so much of my life trying not to need anyone or anything, but I don't want to go on without her. I need her."

"I trusted you. Then you go behind my back and pull something like this?" Miles shook his head. "You're dead to me, man."

The worst had happened. I'd lost the woman I loved and betrayed a member of the found family I'd created since I'd been on my own. Nothing else could cause me the same pain. If Emma rejected me, at least I'd know I'd tried.

"I hope we'll find a way past this someday." I grabbed the coat I'd tossed over the side of his couch and let myself out. It was too late to leave tonight, plus I needed to figure out what to do with Moose if I was going to make the twenty-plus hour drive down to Southern California.

With a heaviness in my heart, I pulled out of the drive, hoping the friendship Miles and I had built over the past fifteen years would be able to withstand this.

IT HAD BEEN forty-eight hours since I left Jackson's cabin, and I could still feel his absence like a deep, gut-wrenching ache. I'd never had my heart broken before and wondered how long the pain would last. I wasn't sure how long I could go on feeling like a piece of me was missing.

I stood in front of my door and locked up my apartment for the last time. Everything I hadn't sold online over the past two days fit into my two-door hatchback. I didn't need much at Mom and Dad's and planned on using the funds I'd raised by selling my stuff to pay off my credit card.

The only thing left to do was turn in my keys at the office before I tucked my tail and drove the short distance to the home I grew up in. I stepped to the railing overlooking the grassy area outside my apartment. The view wasn't much—didn't come close to the scenery on display from Jackson's bedroom window—but I'd miss it.

I squinted at a patch of something blue. Looked like someone had stretched a big tarp over the grass. While I tried to decide whether I should head over and say something or leave it since I technically didn't even live in the complex anymore, a man came around the corner of the building with a huge ice chest in his hands. He had on a backward baseball cap and a long sleeve, plaid flannel shirt that made me suck in a breath. If I didn't know any better, I'd say he was a dead ringer for Jackson.

My pulse spiked. Ever since I left Mustang Mountain, I kept expecting to see Jackson somewhere. Run into him on the sidewalk or pass him on the stairs. It was ridiculous... probably just my subconscious trying to work him out of my system. But the man three stories below had the same broad shoulders, the same scruff on his cheeks.

He looked up and caught me staring at him. "Hey, Angel."

I had to grip the railing to keep from falling over. "Jackson? What are you doing here?"

"I was hoping we could talk."

"But I left you in Montana." I did leave him in Montana, didn't I? I pinched my arm to make sure I wasn't dreaming.

"You did. Then got my head out of my ass and followed you home." He set the cooler down and put up his palm. "Don't move, I'm coming up."

I couldn't move if I wanted to. My feet seemed frozen in place. I could hear him taking the steps two or three at a time. Any second he'd appear on the stairs, and I didn't know what I'd say to him.

"Emma." He walked over to me, larger than life, and held out his arms.

Without thinking, I buried myself against his chest and wrapped my arms around him. If this was a dream, I didn't want to wake up. His chest was solid under my cheek. I inhaled huge gulps of his scent. He was here. He'd come after me. But why?

He ran a hand over my hair. "I'm so sorry. I never should have left you."

"What about Miles?" I mumbled against his shirt. It felt too good to be cradled in his embrace to pull away, even for a moment.

"I told him how I feel about you. He didn't take it well, but I'm hoping he'll come around."

"What exactly did you say?" I needed to know how he felt about me. I was ready to go all-in with my mountain man, but what if he didn't feel the same?

He pulled back just far enough to look down at me and hold my gaze. "I told him I love you. That I don't want to spend another moment without you. I know the isolated life I have in Mustang Mountain might not be what you want."

"What do you mean? I love it there. I love you. Wherever you are is where I want to be."

"Do you mean it?"

I stared deep into his eyes and saw the love I felt for him reflected back at me. "With all my heart."

"Then I've got something to ask you." He swept me up in his arms and carried me down three flights of stairs.

I clung to his shoulders while I bounced against his chest. "What are you doing? Put me down."

"Not until I show you what I've been working on." He reached the stairwell at the bottom of the steps and tugged me toward the big, blue tarp. "Close your eyes and don't open them until I tell you to."

"What did you do?" I laughed as I put my hands over my face.

The fabric rustled as I stood there, then Jackson was back at my side. "Okay, you can open them."

I blinked against the sun and focused on the patch of snow he'd had covered with the tarp. "Where did you find snow in San Diego?"

"I brought it with me. Now read what it says before it melts."

He must have used his boots to stomp out the letters he formed in the small patch of snow. I could make out four words. Four words that on their own didn't mean much, but when strung together the way he'd written them, could only mean one thing.

"Will you marry me?" I read the words out loud with my heart pounding so loudly I was afraid the entire apartment complex could hear it.

Jackson got down on his knee and held out a small

blue velvet box. "Please say yes, Emma. Will you marry me?"

"Yes. Of course, I'll marry you."

He opened the box to reveal a gorgeous diamond set in a platinum band. "You just made me the happiest man alive; do you know that?"

"From grumpiest to happiest, that's quite a change." I let him slip the ring onto my finger and marveled at the way the stone reflected the light.

"I guess that's what you do to me. I'll have to hand over the title of grumpiest man in Mustang Mountain to someone else." He wrapped his arms around me and nuzzled his chin into my neck. "I love you so much. Thank you for saying yes."

"I could never refuse you. But what possessed you to haul snow all the way from Montana to San Diego?"

"You said you liked it. I was hoping it would remind you of the time we spent together... of me rescuing you in the snow."

"That's when I fell in love with you." I nudged my nose against his. "Do you remember when it was that you fell in love with me?"

He slid his hands into the back pocket of my jeans and stared down at me. "I'm pretty sure I fell in love with you the first time I saw you."

"That was years ago." I bumped against him.

"I know. You've had my heart for over a decade, you just didn't know it. Now, what do I need to do so I can take you home?"

"I probably should stop in and tell my parents I'm

not moving in with them and that I got engaged." I arched my brows and waited to see how he'd respond to sharing the news so soon.

"Of course. Do you think your dad will be pissed I didn't ask for his blessing first?"

My parents loved Jackson like a son. I couldn't imagine them being anything but thrilled for both of us after they got over the initial surprise. "I think they'll be very happy to welcome you into the family. Though maybe we can wait a little while before we head over."

"What do you have in mind?"

I pulled the keys to my empty apartment out of my pocket. "Shouldn't we celebrate the fact we just got engaged?"

He took the keys from me and tugged me toward the stairs. "We need to hurry. Moose is in the truck and patience isn't one of her strengths."

We raced up the steps, ready to start a new life together. A life in the rugged hills of Mustang Mountain. I couldn't wait to get back there with the man I'd spend the rest of my life with.

I couldn't wait to get home.

EPILOGUE
FORD

THE BELL JINGLED over the diner's door, causing me to look up. My buddy Jackson walked in. I assumed the woman with him was Miles's sister, Emma. I knew he went to San Diego after her, but I hadn't heard from him since. I didn't even know they were back in town already. Seeing how he had his arm wrapped around the curvy blonde, I'd be willing to guess he had good news.

Jackson waved, then said something to Emma before he led her back to the table I chose at the far end of the diner. He nodded to a few people along the way before they both slid into the booth across from me.

"I take it things went well." I nodded toward Emma.

They looked at each other and smiled.

"We're engaged!" Emma held out her hand. A pretty impressive rock sat on her ring finger.

"Congratulations," I said, not sure how else to

respond. I wished Luna was with me. She was so much better with girly stuff like this. She always knew what to say and would probably gush over the ring, ask all the right questions, and make Emma feel right at home. That's what made us such great friends, since she could do all those things I couldn't.

"Jackson needs to introduce you to Luna. She teaches kindergarten here, and she can get you all set up with wedding details and who to talk to around town," I offered.

"Luna is Ford's best friend. They grew up in Mustang Mountain together." Jackson put his arm around his new fiancée while he filled in some missing details.

"I can't wait to meet her. Oh, there's Ruby. I'll be back in a minute." Emma popped up and headed over to chat with Ruby.

"Seeing how things worked out with you and Emma, Ruby's going to be even more determined to get the rest of us matched up. You know she'll take credit for that," I said. Jackson showed me the flyers Ruby put up around town, and I still had one of the postcards she'd sent out.

"I know she will, and I came to terms with that on my drive to San Diego to try to win Emma back. I suppose it's a small price to pay," he said.

"A small price for you that the rest of us will be paying for, for who knows how long." I grunted and sipped my coffee.

"We'll figure it out at the next meeting." Jackson

stood and held out his hand. "I'm going to catch up with Emma. It was good to see you, Ford."

I shook his hand, then watched him walk over to join Emma. The way they looked at each other made my stomach twist. Not because I don't want what they have, because I do. It's just the woman I want that with will never want me.

After the sweet taste of success, Ruby was bound to double down on her efforts to match the rest of us up. I sure as hell didn't want to have pictures of me all over town.

I glanced over at Jackson and Emma again and caught Ruby staring at me with a look I couldn't read. I didn't like that look. I didn't like it one bit.

I finished my coffee and left enough to cover the tab and the tip on the table. Seemed like a good time to sneak out while Jackson and Emma had Ruby distracted. Of course, that's when my phone rang.

"Hello?"

"Ford. My house has been broken into!" A panicked Luna greeted me from the other end of the line.

"Luna, calm down. What do you mean, your house has been broken into?" I raised my voice, which of course caught Jackson's attention. He looked over at me, his brows arched.

"Someone threw a rock through my window and my stuff is all over the place inside." She sounded like she was on the verge of tears.

My pulse skyrocketed. If anyone hurt her, they'd

have to deal with me. "Get back in your car and lock the door. Call the police. I'm leaving the diner now and will be there in just a few minutes."

Jackson covered the distance to the door in a few long strides. "I'm going with you."

"Emma can stay here with me while you boys go take care of Luna." Ruby shooed us out the door, but not before Jackson pulled Emma close for a kiss.

"First Ruby's hare-brained scheme and now a break-in. What the hell is happening to Mustang Mountain?" I didn't wait for an answer. The sooner I could get to Luna, the better I'd feel.

Want to read more about Jackson and Emma? Get a free bonus scene here: http://subscribepage.io/ DeQyGk.

The next two mountain men of Mustang Mountain are waiting for you!

February is for Ford - https://www.matchofthe monthbooks.com/February-Ford

March is for Miles - https://www.matchofthemon thbooks.com/March-Miles

MOUNTAIN MEN OF MUSTANG MOUNTAIN

Welcome to Mustang Mountain where love runs as wild as the free-spirited horses who roam the hillsides. Framed by rivers, lakes, and breathtaking mountains, it's also the place the Mountain Men of Mustang Mountain call home. They might be rugged and reclusive, but they'll risk their hearts for the curvy girls they love.

To learn more about the Mountain Men of Mustang Mountain, visit our website (https://www.matchofthe monthbooks.com/) join our newsletter here (http://subscribepage.io/MatchOfTheMonth) or follow our Patreon here (https://www.patreon.com/MatchOfThe Month)

January is for Jackson - https://www.matchofthe monthbooks.com/January-Jackson

February is for Ford - https://www.matchofthe monthbooks.com/February-Ford

March is for Miles - https://www.matchofthemon thbooks.com/March-Miles

ACKNOWLEDGMENTS

A huge, heartfelt thanks goes to everyone who's supported us in our writing, especially our HUSSIES of Mountain Men of Mustang Mountain patrons:

Jackie Ziegler

To learn more about the Mountain Men of Mustang Mountain on Patreon, visit us here: https://www.patreon.com/MatchOfTheMonth

Mountain Men of Mustang Mountain Series

January is for Jackson

March is for Miles

Whiskey Wars Series

Drinking Deep

Tasting Temptation

Sipping Seduction

Tying the Knot in Texas Series

The Cowboy Says I Do

Her Kind of Cowboy

Crazy About a Cowboy

Lovebird Café Series

Lemon Tarts & Stolen Hearts

Sweet Tea & Second Chances

Mud Pies & Family Ties

Hot Fudge & a Heartthrob

Holiday, Texas Series

All-American Cowboy

Cowboy Christmas Jubilee

Cowboy Charming

The Love Vixen Series

Getting Lucky in Love

Standalone Romances

All I Wanna Do Is You

ALSO BY EVE LONDON

Lonestar Riders MC Series*

One Night Series*

Matched with a Mountain Man Series**

Claimed by a Cowboy Series**

Summer Lovin' Series

Shared Series

January is for Jackson - Mountain Men of Mustang Mountain

One Night with a Diver* - Love on the Sunshine Coast Series

Hot Diggity Dogs* - Love at First Bark Series

Hot Drummer Summer* - Hot HEA Summer Series

One Night with a SEAL* - SEAL Team Romeo

Mustard Been You* - Sycamore Mountain Man of the Month Club

Hearts on Fire* - Hearts, Flames, and Hoses Series

Beaded by Midnight* - World's Biggest Party Series

Romancing the Quarterback* - Galentine's Getaway Series

Dating the Cowboy* - Matchmakers, Inc. Series

Kiss Off Countdown* - Midnight Kisses Series

Codename: Wolf* - Soldiers for Christmas Series

Room Twenty-Four - Club Sin Series

Dangerous Curves* - Curvy Soulmates Series

Trick or Tequila** - Halloween Steam Series

Single Dad Dilemma - Starlight Bay Series

* Features one of Mama Mae's boys as the hero

** Ties to one of Mama Mae's boys

ABOUT DYLANN CRUSH

USA Today bestselling author Dylann Crush writes contemporary romance with sizzle, sass, heart and humor. A true romantic, she loves her heroines spunky and her heroes super sexy. When she's not dreaming up steamy storylines, she can be found sipping a margarita and searching for the best Tex-Mex food in the Upper Midwest.

Dylann co-hosts Romance Happy Hour (https://www.romancehappyhour.com/) with live episodes every 2nd and 4th Thursday of each month and is the founder of Book Box Babe (https://www.BookBoxBabe.com) where readers can find hand-curated, romance novel themed subscription boxes, and specialty items.

Although she grew up in Texas, she currently lives in a suburb of Minneapolis/St. Paul with her unflappable husband, three energetic kids, a clumsy Great Dane, a lovable rescue mutt, a very chill cat, and a crazy kitten. She loves to connect with readers, other authors and fans of tequila.

You can find her at www.dylanncrush.com.

facebook.com/dylanncrush

instagram.com/dylanncrush

pinterest.com/dylanncrush

bookbub.com/authors/dylann-crush

goodreads.com/DylannCrush

tiktok.com/@dylanncrush

ABOUT EVE LONDON

When Eve London was a girl she wanted to be a trapeze artist. Instead, she grew up to be like most women—a juggler—trying to keep bunches of balls in the air.

Now she spends her days writing about the kind of men she likes – sexy, shameless, and just a little bit sarcastic.

www.EveLondonAuthor.com

facebook.com/evelondonauthor

instagram.com/evelondonbooks

bookbub.com/authors/eve-london

patreon.com/EveLondon

Made in the USA
Monee, IL
12 December 2024